A NOTE TO PARENTS

Congratulations on choosing the best ... . .s for your child. By selecting top-quality McGraw-Hill products, you can be assured that the concepts used in our books will reinforce and enhance the skills that are being taught in classrooms nationwide.

And what better way to get young readers excited than with Mercer Mayer's Little Critter, a character loved by children everywhere? Our First Readers offer simple and engaging stories about Little Critter that children can read on their own. Each level incorporates reading skills, colorful illustrations, and challenging activities.

Level 1 – The stories are simple and use repetitive language. Illustrations are highly supportive.
Level 2 - The stories begin to grow in complexity. Language is still repetitive, but it is mixed with more challenging vocabulary.
Level 3 - The stories are more complex. Sentences are longer and more varied.

To help your child make the most of this book, look at the first few pictures in the story and discuss what is happening. Ask your child to predict where the story is going. Then, once your child has read the story, have him or her review the word list and do the activities. This will reinforce vocabulary words from the story and build reading comprehension.

You are your child's first and most influential teacher. No one knows your child the way you do. Tailor your time together to reinforce a newly acquired skill or to overcome a temporary stumbling block. Praise your child's progress and ideas, take delight in his or her imagination, and most of all, enjoy your time together!

Library of Congress Cataloging-in-Publication Data

Mayer, Mercer, 1943-
    A yummy lunch / by Mercer Mayer.
        p. cm. — (First readers, skills and practice)
    Summary: Little Critter makes Mom his famous peanut butter, pickle, potato chips, and orange juice
sandwich for lunch. Includes activities.
    ISBN 1-57768-809-0
      [1. Sandwiches Fiction.] I. Title. II. Series.

PZ7.M462 Yu 2001
[E] dc21
                                                      2001031210

McGraw-Hill
Children's Publishing

A Division of The **McGraw·Hill** Companies

Send all inquiries to:
McGraw-Hill Children's Publishing
8787 Orion Place
Columbus, OH 43240-4027

Printed in the United States of America.

1-57768-809-0

1 2 3 4 5 6 7 8 9 10 PHXBK 06 05 04 03 02 01

 A Big Tuna Trading Company, LLC/J. R. Sansevere Book

FIRST READERS

Level 2   Grades K - 1

A YUMMY LUNCH

by Mercer Mayer

Mc Graw Hill **McGraw-Hill**
Children's Publishing

Columbus, Ohio

I am going to make lunch for Mom.
First, I need some bread.

Then, I need some peanut butter
to spread on the bread.

Then, I need some pickles to put on top of the peanut butter.

Then, I need some potato chips
to cover the pickles.

10

Then, I need some orange juice
to pour on the potato chips.

"Mom! Lunch is ready. I made my famous peanut butter and pickle sandwiches with potato chips and orange juice!" I say.

I think Mom really likes her lunch.
She says it is so good, that she wants
to share it with Dad!

Word List

Read each word in the list below. Then, find it in the story. Now, make up a new sentence using the word. Say your sentence out loud.

Words I Know
bread
peanut butter
pickles
potato chips
orange juice

Challenge Words
going
lunch
ready
famous
sandwiches

How Does It Taste?

Pretend that you just tasted Little Critter's famous peanut butter and pickle sandwich. Draw a picture of your face to show what it would look like. Then, write what you would say to answer Little Critter's question.

How does it taste?

What You Would Say

Your Face

Action Words

Circle the action words below.

hug

dig

sandwich

dogs

run

Make a New Word

Change one letter of the word fall to make a new word that goes with the picture.

fall ⟶ ___ball___

Change one letter of the word hug to make a new word that goes with the picture.

hug ⟶ ___bug___

Change one letter of the word camp to make a new word that goes with the picture.

camp ⟶ ___lamp___

What Happened?

In what order did Little Critter put together the food to make Mom's sandwich? Write the ordinal number from the number bank in the box under each food. Try not to look back at the story.

Number Bank
1st
2nd
3rd
4th

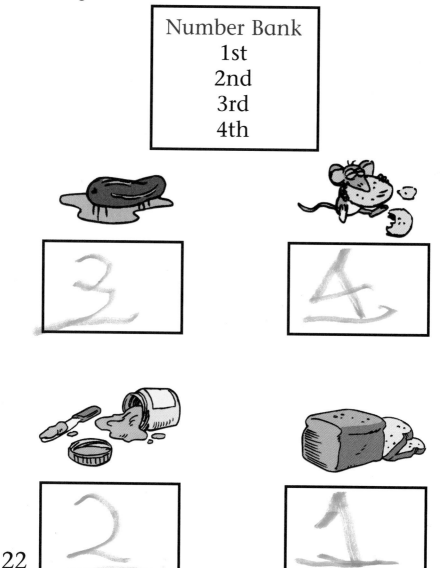

Word Families

Words come in word families. A word family is a group of words that has the same ending sound. Below are some words in two different word families. Add some more words to each word family.

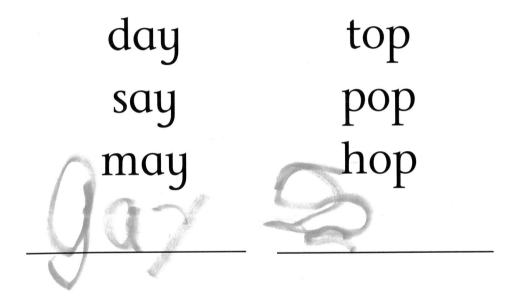

day	top
say	pop
may	hop

_____   _____

_____   _____

_____   _____

_____   _____

Answer Key

page 19
How Does It Taste?

Answers will vary.

page 20
Action Words

hug

dig

sandwich

dogs

run

page 21
Make a New Word

Change one letter of the word fall to make a new word that goes with the picture.

fall → __ball__

Change one letter of the word hug to make a new word that goes with the picture.

hug → __bug__

Change one letter of the word camp to make a new word that goes with the picture.

camp → __lamp__

page 22
What Happened?

| 3rd | 4th |

| 2nd | 1st |

page 23
Word Families

Sample answers given below.

hay	mop
bay	hop
pay	stop
ray	shop
lay	cop